FOR THE LOVE OF CHARLIE

By: Rebecca Anne Moll

This book is dedicated to the memory of Rita Marie Melanson and Charles Wilfrid Boudreau. May God bless you both as you have blessed us.

For my Mother and Father, with Love.

Table of Contents

ANNIE

A Mother's Fate

It was a beautiful summer morning to be in the fields. The sun was rising, making little diamonds of dew line up like soldiers at attention. Not a leaf was moving, so silent was the wind. Nova Scotia mornings were the kind that made you feel grounded to the land and one of the reasons Frank could never live anywhere else. Taking a deep breath in he let the cool air tickle the back of his throat and fill his lungs. Annie, he thought, was pleasant and surprising like that, and just thinking of her he began to smile. Today was to be filled with hours in the field, the tomatoes and beans were almost ready and the corn had to be checked for worms. When the crops came in it was all work and with the unpredictable weather of downeast you couldn't wait a day or a surprise storm could wipe out everything.

Typical of French Canadian men, Frank was small of frame, quite angular in the face, and lean to the bone. His complexion was dark and his hair unruly, cut as short as respectable could be. Thick and wavy, his habit was to push it off his face leaving a wave of sorts, similar to the very fields he worked. He pulled his cap down further over his eyes, squared his shoulders and headed out leading Betsy, which is no small feat in itself. Not much led Betsy, obstinate old oxen; God only knows how old she was. Seems Frank couldn't think of a time when he wasn't persuading her to move. She was his Daddy's favorite and when he took over the farm she was a blessing. Digging fields was hard, backbreaking work and without her his lot would be far less and much harder.

As the sun became fuller a heat began to penetrate the air and a smooth easy wind brushed against his face, he thought about the generations of Melanson men that had worked these fields and the women that tended the homes. It was hard to believe his fortune. First, Annie, she was his prize; sometimes he wondered how she could ever love him. Second, the land, this was prime farming land with high enough ground to drain, but close enough to the water to draw in moisture. Caught between the bay and the hills the updrafts pulled in the very salt of the sea over the bay and across his farm. It had a sprinkling effect that made everything thrive and grow. Last, but not the least in anyway, was Rita; his new baby girl. How soon they were blessed with a family! Annie had dealt with the trials of pregnancy in typical Crispo fashion – staunch, but observant. She tended her chores and helped in the fields until the last few weeks. Being with child made her so beautiful and yet somehow now as a mother she was even more so.

Annie and Frank grew up together, just houses apart. In this area, most spouses knew each other as children, as families celebrated holidays and birthdays, weddings, and funerals together. Sunday mass and Saturday night fiddle dances brought the clans together. The Trudeaus, Labatts, Richards and many others helped each other, lending a sense of familiarity only such a community can foster. Yet, although he had pulled her hair as a toddler and they had chased each other through the corn for endless summers of hide and seek, when Annie became a woman he found himself, well beside himself.

Annie had gone away that spring to stay with her Aunt Durilda in Halifax. It was a busy time helping his father with the planting and he hadn't given her much thought. He had heard she was learning dressmaking and may become an apprentice in her aunt's boutique. Halifax was a world away with its city streets and cobblestone sidewalks and hundreds of people. He had been there once on a holiday and found the noise constant and unsettling. He couldn't sleep at night for all the conversations replaying in his head and once home again never thought to return. So when Annie came back that June he didn't plan to pay her much attention. But, he couldn't help but pay attention. Small and shy as a girl with long pigtails of auburn hair she resembled so many of the French Canadian girls. Halifax had watched her transformation and thus deposited in his midst the most beautiful woman he had ever seen. The once long and plain auburn hair was radiant and rich in neat piles upon her head. Her neck was slim and fair, lending a tilt to her chin and raise to the brow that allowed one to fall into her endless eyes of green. Small in stature she stood a few inches shorter than he. She was confident, yet polite, and managed herself in a way that some take years to achieve. He felt lost. Lost in her presence and lost that she would return to Halifax.

Yet, Annie sought him out. They went for long walks in the evenings and she told him all about the city. She took quickly to dressmaking and her aunt had offered her a full position in the fall after harvest. Frank listened and his heart sank. He knew he would never leave this place, yet how lonely he would be without Annie. He couldn't imagine life without either. The summer passed quickly like a session of stills in a movie. Frank and Annie grew closer and fell in love. Autumn approached and cool air began to accompany their evening walks. One night while returning from the wharf Frank wrapped his coat around her shoulders and his arms around her heart.

"Annie, will you stay with me, raise a family, be my partner and my love, and grow old with me?"

To which she replied, "Merci, I thought you would never ask!"

With his thoughts in the clouds and his determination willed on Betsy, Frank moved over the crest and towards the beans. He needed to check the lines and make sure they were trailing. The sound of seagulls echoing songs washed over with the wind as well as a smattering of words from a neighboring conversation. Annie would be going out to the barn about now, he thought. It was time for the baby to sleep and she would want to get the lamps filled. Dangerous work, Annie never tended the oil lamps with Rita around, or in the house. The wells had to be filled with oil, wicks trimmed and set so it was safe to light in the house. This was work best done undistracted. Annie liked to be outside and preferred doing so in the yard, but with the breeze up lately, the wicks wouldn't light.

Frank crouched down next to the beans and began working. He liked the way the rows enveloped you in a tent of sorts, a lattice covering that let in light and shadow at odds. He heard a cricket call out and the blast of a ship leaving the harbor. The faint sound of a cow bellowing and the snort of Betsy two rows over pitched in. The wind had picked up to a steady blow, cooling the sweat that had settled under his cap.

Suddenly, his name was called. It was urgent and it was Annie. Not one to call out, he knew there was something wrong and he felt his panic rise. His mind raced for an explanation as his feet tore across the fields towards the barn. Pumping blood through his veins and adrenaline through his brain his mind worked over itself pushing his feet through the thick soil. A flash he saw at the door to the barn and doors blow open and close in the wind. Bright red fabric tinged in gold, crimson, twirling in the wind – Annie's dress and what else? He reached the barn as she ran into his arms screaming, flames and char, tears, and despair. The smell of kerosene and fire engulfed his senses. Thrown to the ground he wrapped his coat around them and rolled over and over as her screams hollowed out his ears and grabbed hold of his thoughts.

"My Annie, my Annie", he cried.

The heat that tore at his legs subsided. The wind slackened to a small breeze. Annie lay still, her hair in his face, her arms around his head. Her screaming became faint, almost a whisper. Frank rolled over, pushed her hair away and closed her eyes, looking as she did that morning before waking. Her whisper still in his ears he felt the anguish of shock and life's betrayal. She can't be gone – oh Annie, my Annie. Lying there, his mind sought life to explain the cries that echoed in his ears, the sound becoming louder and louder, no longer a cry of pain or despair, but of need. He shook Annie's lifeless body, a feeble attempt to restore life and cried "If you must go, don't torment me with your cries." His eyes, filled with tears, tore open as he realized the source of the sound – not his beloved Annie, but with all the cruelty and harshness of life – *Rita.*

CHARLIE

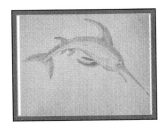

Big Beginnings

It was a record birth for the annals of Isle Madam, a record temperature too. January 25, 1912 registered the mercury just below -10 F and the largest birth ever recorded at 11 pounds 6 ounces.

"Twins." said Mrs. Donovan, the local midwife.

"All in the front and nothing in the back is a boy for sure." declared Alice Marie, sister and assistant to the midwife.

Of course, opinions varied throughout the community of D'Escousse, Nova Scotia, as often women do. Some always acted with pure conviction and others contrary just to esteem themselves apart from others as an expert. Regardless of opinion, Minnie Boudreau knew this was no normal pregnancy and impending birth either. Her third child, each increasing in length and weight, she knew she was in for a hell of a fight with this one or these ones. She also knew she was going to bolt the bedroom door for from now on; another baby would be the death of her, no doubt.

Located in the Canadian Maritimes, Isle Madame, a small island off the southeast corner of Cape Breton, Nova Scotia was the home to many of the Boudreau descendents. Close-knit communities such as Poulamon and D'Escousse, to Arichat and the far reaches of Petit-De-Grat and Sampson's cove were founded on hard work, faith in God, and the love of the sea. Originating from ten Acadian families that fled Port Toulouse (St. Peter's) after the fall of Louisburg in 1748, hailed as the pivotal battle in the French and Indian War, it was a tight knit community with more in common than bloodlines. Although allegiant to the crown of England, the Acadians, having evolved from true French settlers, were a clannish crowd with their own dialect, customs, and traditions that were no longer French or English. Theophil, Minnie's husband, was born & raised on Boudreau Island, located just off the coast of Poulamon. It looked a hard and desolate place to raise a family, Minnie thought, with nothing but towering evergreens and the constant threat of wind and water surrounding you. It was a good thing Theo decided to settle in D'Escousse; she would be in a real pickle now if she was stuck on that island.

Around midnight on the 24th her labor pains started. No novice to this, Minnie put some tea on to brew and began walking throughout the house, hoping not to wake the children or Theo. Theo had been up just 'til the hour before securing the barn, amongst other things. The skies had looked as if they were frozen themselves, just to be spiteful, denying access to the sun all day. A sure sign for snow and lots of it, she thought. The pressure was dropping and from all accounts, it had the making a real January nor'easter. Winters on the island were harsh and babies were born regardless. Minnie thought she'd wait until daylight, and then send Cliff out for the midwife. Cliff was her eldest, and though only ten years old, he worked the fields with his father like a man. He was responsible like one too. Not like Eddie, her second son, he would get lost going to the barn and back, forget what he out there for and find something else more to his liking to do. So different these boys, it made Minnie wonder about the third one soon to come. Maybe it will be a little of both. Theo says hopefully more of the first. Minnie was hoping for a girl until she got so big and Mrs. Donovan fashioned her belt to support her belly. No girl should be this big, Minnie thought. A baby this big should be a boy – what a worker he'd be!

Around 5 o'clock in the morning the pains were getting closer and stronger. She went to get Theo, figuring he'd need some time to send Cliff for the midwife and get himself out to the barn. There was no need to bother Eddie, he would sleep through anything and he was more useful asleep than awake when it came to birthing babies. Stopping to allow each contraction to subside, Minnie crept into the bedroom. It was so dark; it took a moment for her eyes to adjust. Theo had to sleep in total darkness. Even a little light would keep the man awake for hours. When they were first married, she made drapes out of old sheets and a woolen blanket. It kept what little heat they had in the house and what little light of the moon out. When Theo saw the drapes he said "My God woman, I'm not much for housekeeping, but there are some man curtains for sure." Minnie reached her hand down and rested it on Theo's cheek. She felt the outline and strength of his jaw. The cold of her hand was all it took to wake him.

"What is it, Minnie? Is it the baby?"

A nod of her head and he was pulling on his clothes and reaching for his boots under the bed.

"I'll get Cliff out right away," He said.

"Are you okay?" he asked.

"I'm managing, but this one is a fast mover," Minnie replied.

With help on the way, Minnie eased herself into the bed.

"Go on, Theo," She said. "Go check the stove, too. It's been awhile since I added wood."

Cliff ran into the wind, head down, along the edges on the fence until he got to the creek. His lanky arms and legs looked like pinwheels splaying out as he tried to keep from falling in the snow. The creek was frozen solid; it seemed like another world when they waded here just a few months ago. Cliff loved summer and hated the winter. Being the oldest was hard work and even harder in the winter. He dreamed of places warm, like Florida or California. He knew someday he'd move away from the cold northeast and head south. There was always a job for a hard worker and at least he wouldn't freeze down south. Sometimes late at night he'd read to Eddie out of the encyclopedia about all the warm places they could go. They'd own a fishing boat they could sleep on and travel from port to port, catching fish and selling them. Cliff would run the charts and Eddie the lines, for Cliff was the leader and Eddie the follower. Dad liked to say Eddie would follow anyone, as long as they had food and it didn't require too much work. That Eddie, he sure was a dreamer, Cliff mused. Half the time he was off somewhere else staring at God knows what. Mom says he gonna need a real good woman with a real short leash when he gets to marrying. Like tonight, running to get the midwife. Eddie could never do that – he'd come back after the baby was born and ask "what was it you wanted?" Cliff knew his work was harder because Eddie never pulled his weight, but something about his brother wouldn't let the anger rise up in him. It was like he needed to protect him, like it was his job.

Crossing the creek, Cliff jumped over the fence and into Mr. Donovan's pasture. Two more fences and he'd be at the house. Taking the road might seem easier, less snow to cover; but the road ran with the sea and by the time he made it around the inlet and back to the Donovan's the sun would be rising, not to mention the gale off the coast fighting you the whole way. Mrs. Donovan birthed just about every baby in the area and if they were born before she began birthing, then her mother did the favor. He guessed it went back for at least three or four generations, maybe even to birthing on the boats that brought them here from across the ocean. On a small Island like Isle Madam, you only needed one midwife; although, sometimes she was mighty busy. Her sister, Alice-Marie, learned alongside of her, but she needed direction in more things than birthing. A full grown woman, Alice Marie still lived with her sister and never married. Mom said she probably never would marry; no man would ever have the patience for her like her sister. Cliff wondered if there was a man with a short leash for her, like Eddie, and had the feeling that Mrs. Donovan felt for Alice Mary like he did for Eddie.

Having jumped the last fence he ran up the steps and gave the door a rattle. Mrs. Donovan was on the other side, dressed and ready. Surprised to see her, he gave a little yell and fell back into the snow.

"Goodness boy, "she said "I'd be foolish not to be at the door on a night like this – perfect weather for birthing babies!"

With that, she gave Cliff a hand, brushed the snow off his back and told him to meet her at the barn. Mr. Donovan had the horses ready and they'd take the wagon over right away. Cliff settled into the seat under a warm quilt, thankful he didn't have to run the way back. His legs were tired and his feet were numb with cold.

"Someday, I'm going live in Florida," he told Mrs. Donovan.

"You do that, Cliff, and you'll have company for sure!" She replied.

All predictions aside, Minnie gave birth to one baby, the size of two. He was a fast and furious delivery and

Minnie knew it was a boy before Mrs. Donovan handed him to her.

"Send him over anytime," Said Mrs. Donovan, "That is, when he's big enough to work. Seems to me, a boy that big could do the work of two."

"There's time enough for that, thank goodness," Minnie said.

"What will you name him?" She asked.

"Charles. Charles Wilfrid Boudrea," Minnie said.

Coming into the room, Theo kissed Minnie on the forehead and peeked into the bundle she held against her. "Well, that's a big name for a baby, Minnie dear, but it looks like it will fit just fine!" he exclaimed.

Yearning for the World Outside

From the time Charlie was a young boy, he was known as Big Charlie. In the years approaching 1920, those who lived on Cape Breton were mostly French Canadian and by normal standards not very big people. A man would stand around 5'4" and his wife maybe 4'10". Charlie grew past the women by the time he was 8 and at 10 years old he was the size of a man. But it wasn't just his height that earned him the nickname, Big Charlie, it was his presence altogether. He was a barrel-chested boy with thick arms & legs, well muscled from working in the fields. Wide across the shoulders, he could hold the yoke of a plow as well as the ox and often this earned him the ability to finish the field in half the time. When a task required pure brute strength, they called upon Big Charlie. Strong as the ox, but more pleasant in disposition, he would do what was asked without hesitation. Minnie & Theo knew Charlie was a blessing for a son, but they also knew that soon he would be looking beyond his boyhood surroundings. As most young men do, he would get restless and want to see more of the world. Already, at the age of 12, he wanted to go to sea.

Growing up in Cape Breton in the early 1920's was a childhood not only of work, but a fair share of fun too. When the winters bore down and adults hovered indoors, Charlie and Eddie fastened sleds out of wood, sanding for days in the barn until the runners were like glass. A mast was made using a fence post and one of Minnie's missing bed sheets, anchored to the middle of the sled with line to release given the conditions and direction of the wind. Tying the sled with ropes to the back of the ox, they'd blindfold the bull to get him out on the ice, being sure to face him away from the shore. With a brother secure on the sled, the other would release the blindfold and give the bull a loud smack on the hindquarter. One look at where he was and the ox would take off running with the sled rider working the sail to gain maximum speed. The brother left behind had no time to catch up, but stayed hands on knees laughing until the bull turned around and charged back to shore. It was a game of adventure and fun whether you were the brother sailing across the ice or other being chased by an angry & frightened ox!

Many years younger, their little sister Blanche would sit by the shore and play lookout. Her job was to run home, should the bull fall through the ice or run over the one who slapped him. It was an occasion or two that she did run for help, her chubby legs and baby steps proceeding in slow-motion, although, by the time Minnie made it down the road to the lake, one boy would be on shore racked with laughter, the other chasing down a mad bull dragging a sailboat made for ice!

Blanche was the darling of the family. Gentle and sweet, she gave Minnie the warm love that hard working boys could not. Minnie knew that it was only time before her full and lively house would be empty and quiet. Already, Cliff had left for the States following love to Boston and Charlie talked only of the sea. Minnie would sit and watch her family at supper time and take solace in Blanche and her need of her mother. Cherub in feature, Blanche's beautiful curls were a mother's dream and they spent many hours together teaching and learning the things only a mother and daughter could share. Fiercely protected by her brothers, Blanche grew up in a loving and secure home that only enhanced her good nature. She was the last of the Boudreau's for Minnie & Theo; a bonus that blessed the entire family.

Living on Isle Madam, there is a constant view of the water. At the highest point, for at least 180 degrees, the view is of water. Like the land and sea, mended together by a seam of shoreline, the people were bound to the land as well as the sea. Netting fish, trapping lobster, farming oysters, and digging clams were just a few of the ways families made their way with the sea. Cultivating both was a way of life, one that had served them well for many years. Theo's brother, Alfred, owned and operated a fishing boat. It was not a small boat, with a galley, bunkhouse, and room for a crew of six, but for a fishing boat it was on the smaller side. Big enough to handle the rip around Cape La Ronde, his Uncle Alfred sailed up and down the Atlantic coast and the *Bras d'Or Lakes,* the large salt water body located in middle of Cape Breton. Charlie dreamed of working the lines and hauling in fish by the thousands. Sent to bed earlier than he felt fair, he'd sit upon the top step and listen to the men tell sea stories around the kitchen table. Fueled by a lively poker game and a few jiggers of rum, the tales went beyond reality, making a home in a young man's heart.

It was a cold and wicked morning when Theo woke Charlie. Darkness enveloped the room, hours before sun-up, it promised to be a gloomy day at best.

"Your Uncle wants you down at the wharf, Charlie. Best get a move on, he leaves with or without ya," Theo said.

Charlie turned to ask a question only to find himself alone and the door ajar. A soft glow, the kitchen stove taking light, was beginning take shape downstairs. He could hear the muffled sound of his mother's skirts as she moved around the kitchen floor. Placing two feet through his pants and then on the floor, Charlie rose and slipped his suspenders over his shoulders. Splashing water on his face from the basin he grabbed his shirt off the peg, buttoning it as he descended the stairs. There wasn't much doubt when Charlie descended the stairs; each step groaning under his oversized boyhood frame, his mother turned with a smile to greet him good morning.

"Cook's gone sick; looks like you're getting what you dreamed of," She said.

Ducking to avoid the beam into the kitchen, Charlie took a seat and began pulling on his boots.

"Better take my oilskins, boy, a cook's bound to be on deck sometime," His father said.

"Thanks Pop," Charlie replied.

"Mind your Uncle and don't do anything foolish, young man," his father said. "You'll be back in thirty days and we want to see ya coming off the boat on your own accord."

"Yes, sir. I love you Mom," He said. "You too, Pop."

He held his mother close for a moment then kissed her on the forehead, bending down to meet her gentle eyes. "See you when the moon's back around." He grinned, gripping his father's hand, feeling the tough and familiar leather of his palm.

Taking one last look around him at this warm and wonderful center of his childhood home, Charlie grabbed his hat off the wall and stepped out the door. With the wind searing his frame, he bent his head down and made his way to the wharf. His large strides fought for footing, making him feel full of purpose, like he was finally going to make his mark on the world. From the safety and security of his home to the wild and violent world of the sea, Charlie would never be the same again, nor would he ever stay on land for long either. For him, the sea was all he needed.

Charting His Course

For those who loved the sea, in the early part of the 20th century, it was not an easy love. Technology was still at least forty years away, leaving a fisherman to his experience, skill, and wits. Weather patterns held limitless change, making the normal tedious task of charting and staying on course even more difficult. Taking a sight with a sextant to give latitude, along with a marine chronometer for longitude, a sailor could determine location. Using a compass for heading, the course was set in degrees N, NW, S, or SE. Even if the fisherman were to stay close to shore for land reference, charting was still wise in case of intruding weather. Keen to learn this trade, Charlie kept vigil to the talk around him. The galley was a fisherman's refuge, often the only place he could discuss the goings on upside. It was a perfect place to learn by listening. Soon Charlie learned by doing. Up on deck the captain was king. Orders were followed or not with serious consequence. Each man knew his task and also knew in not doing his task he let the crew down and endangered their lives. Charlie's relationship with his Uncle had always been an easy one, but here at sea there was no acknowledgement of familial bonds. A hand was a hand, regardless of birth.

Charlie began to move out of the galley and upside with menial tasks. From scrubbing decks and cleaning out scuppers to untangling and retying the endless knots in nets, coiling lines, and preparing bait, he learned it all. Working in earnest, it wasn't long before his duties in the galley were relegated elsewhere and he found himself working alongside the older and more experienced fishermen. A boy the size of a man, with the strength to match and the quick & eager aptitude of youth, there were no complaints from the crew. His good nature and friendly disposition overshadowed the usual grumblings of competition common to any change on deck. Realizing his good fortune, Uncle Alfred made a permanent place for Charlie on the crew, pulling in record amounts of cod until the depression came to the Maritimes and newly imposed fishing restrictions caused deep changes for the next decade.

The difficult economic times of the late 1920's and early 1930's hit the Maritimes especially hard. Emigration to the states was the predominate flow over the border, leaving those left behind with a stagnant economy and an aging workforce. Fisherman, loggers, farmers, and miners made up the main industries of Nova Scotia and most of the adults involved could not read or write. Lack of education only compounded the problem, lending to lower prices for the farmers and fisherman and lower wages for the loggers and miners. Being mostly a catholic providence, God was listening to the endless prayers of his faithful Nova Scotians. Little known to those of Cape Breton, a young boy was mindful of the troubles and was soon to be their savior in the cloth.

Moses Coady grew up, the eldest of twelve, on a farm in the Margaree Valley of Cape Breton, Nova Scotia.

Seeing the emigration and hardships left to those who remained, he vowed to help his fellow countrymen. Graduating from St. Xavier University in 1905 at the top of his class, Coady traveled to Rome where he entered the priesthood, studying theology and philosophy. After his ordination in 1910, he returned to his Alma Mater as a teacher. Education was his weapon in the fight against economic depression. Not limiting his teaching to students alone, Coady offered adults a chance at education too. Study clubs gave fishermen and farmers, miners and loggers the chance to understand what was keeping them poor and the opportunity to come up with possible solutions. Where one fisherman alone could barely manage to survive, now many together could have a chance at success. The next decade belonged to the Antigonish Movement, one born of adult education and co-operative business ventures, a so called pooling of resources and minds. The birth of credit unions and microfinance provided sustainability for the movement moving into and beyond WWII.

One to benefit from Coady's meeting of the minds and venture of co-operatives was the United Maritime Fishermen, a wholesale cooperative for the region's fishermen. Offering strong education to its members, it promoted marketing services that helped fishermen fare better with their catch.

Growing up aboard ship throughout those turbulent economic times, Charlie knew that the straight road to success at sea was to get your captain's license. At 19 years old, Charlie was one of the youngest and most trusted captains in Cape Breton. Boat owners would need a ship brought down to Boston and wanted a strong and responsible captain who could handle not only the seas, but the crew, and those unscrupulous characters you were sure to encounter upon docking. A quick mind for math was needed, especially when a catch was to be weighed and prices haggled. Although only educated to the second grade, Charlie could tally the catch, one that would produce a spreadsheet worthy of today's computer programs, without paper or pencil, faster than the accountants could bang on their trusty ten key adding machines.

It was a mixed bag of opportunities for a young sea captain and Charlie never let an opportunity pass. He sailed ships up the Hudson River, through the St. Lawrence Seaway into the Great Lakes, and down the Atlantic Coast to the Caribbean Islands. A member of the Canadian Merchant Marines, he sailed into China and saw the drowning of baby girls, the horrible result of governmental population control. Fishing took him out to the Grand Banks and over the Flemish Cap where the cold Labrador Current runs the opposite alongside the warm waters of the Gulf Stream. Seated next to each other like older and younger brothers, these two geological characters made for an interesting set of criteria ripe for fishing grounds. The underwater plateaus of the Grand Banks and the mixing of the two opposing streams provided for shallower and warmer waters. Nutrients lifted to the surface, allowed for the richest fishing grounds in history, ripe with cod, halibut, sword fish, scallop and lobster. Sailing to the east to fish the Flemish Cap, a captain would follow the unique clockwise current direction, sailing around the Cap, reaping in a bounty of unbelievable proportions.

Geologically, the Grand Banks was a fisherman's dream in terms of fish; however, meteorologically, it could be his nightmare in terms of weather. Opposing currents so great for the catch, could also produce fog so thick it took nerves of steel and a boatload of faith for a captain to sail these waters. It was this thick of fog that gave Charlie the experience of a lifetime. Lost in the dory was a phrase a fisherman never wanted to say or hear, let alone experience.

LOST IN THE DORY

It was a typical trip out to the Banks for the crisp, blustery month of October. Cod were the target this time of year and lining the method. A stiff breeze kept Charlie and the rest of the crew nervous enough to be mindful. Gulls swooned over the bridge calling in a chorus whose harmony was lost on the winds. Sailing to the far edge of the fishing grounds the Captain reversed the course, so the lines could be set and fish hauled in the same fashion. The first hooks set were the first hauled, finishing up on a direction towards home. Dories were set to sea with two men, hooks, line, and bait. The man at the bow of the dory led the line in a bow to stern fashion to the other at the stern, who attached a baited lanyard and fell it to sea. Weights on the hooks allowed the line to drop into the clear blue waters so loved by the fish. Caulked barrels set at regular intervals along the line allowed for flotation and visibility of the rig. Quick work this was, and even on land it would be a challenge to do so without injury. With the added uncertainty of the sea, not to mention its' threateningly cold proximity from the dory, it was a very difficult and dangerous job.

Charlie had signed on as first mate just over a month ago. He knew of the captain, and upon meeting him the first time, agreed with the general consensus of his character and birth name: Bastardache. A stern and serious man, given to temper, he was well respected and revered as a captain who protected his crew and ship above the catch. Not all captains were this way. In greedy attempts to pull in high market catches, many captains lost sight of their crews' safety and subsequently their ship and themselves. Memorialized in stone, their names were a testament to the power and unpredictability of greed, as well as Mother Nature. The task of each crew member was decided from the beginning. Before leaving shore, while provisions for the long months ahead were being loaded into the hold, the captain went over his crew list and keeping in mind the good and bad of each man both skill and moral, he placed each member to a task and a partner. New crew members were often placed with more experienced for obvious reasons, with the exception of those tasks that were not worked together, but in series, such as those of the galley, general deck work, and steering. The first mate oversaw the day to day activities of sailing and fishing, keeping the captain abreast of any circumstances that needed his particular attention.

In the past, due to his years of experience and a good reputation, Charlie was usually paired with those who needed his guidance. The captain called the crew to deck and gave his instructions.

"Here are the assignments until I tell you different," He said.

Listing off positions and names paired he was about half way through the list when he came to Charlie's name. A look of consternation came across his face. He looked up at Charlie and held his gaze steady. Pulling the pencil from his pocket, he gave a quick lick to the tip and made an even and quick stroke across the paper. He looked up again and raised his eyes to the heavens as if looking for assistance. Lowering them to once again meet with Charlie he said,

"Dory – Boudreau, Ouellette." Not expecting to hear his name paired, Charlie was surprised.

As he listened to the rest being called, Charlie wondered about this sudden change. Most likely, it didn't mean anything; he worked the dory hundreds of times, without incident. But recently, he had been 2nd in command at the helm. With a love for both sailing and fishing, Charlie found either task to his liking. Sure the sailing paid more, but what gave him over to sailing more than fishing lately was the power of being responsible for so many. It was in his nature to be a protector and a dream to one day captain his own ship.

Holding to the back of the crowd, he made his way up the plank to the deck last. Captain Bastardasche was greeting the crew as they came aboard. Charlie gripped his captain's hand firmly and said "Good Day, Captain."

"As to you, Boudreau, welcome aboard and don't be worrying 'bout the wages, you'll be getting the first mate pay."

Knowing the captain would never explain or appreciate an inquiry; Charlie nodded his head and made his way aboard. Soon enough he'd learn about his partner and sometime later realize the captain's intuition for putting them together. For now, he set his sights on getting on with this crew.

Like the status and resentful separation of a white and blue collar workforce, the fishing crew and those in command (captain and first mate) were often at odds or at least knew their respective places. The crew sought out each other and bonds were formed as best as possible, given the close proximity and somewhat temperamental qualities of fisherman. Those in command had an easier time of getting on as their experience and maturity gave them the self-confidence to be comfortable in the presence of others who maybe more or less than themselves.

Charlie knew from experience that he needed to set things right from the start with his partner. He never met this Ouellette before and from what he saw, he was a little perplexed as to why he was paired so. Louis Ouellette was at least 40 years his senior. He carried himself like a well seasoned fisherman, was easy to approach, and agreeable to working with Charlie. He had expected a young boy new to the dory or possibly an older, but maybe indisposed man, say one prone to too much drinking.

Making his way below, he saw at the bottom, his partner.

"There you are sir," Charlie said extending his hand to meet Ouellette. "Good day and glad to fish with you; Boudreau's the name."

Ouellette looked up at Charlie and said "No need for sir, Louie is just fine." Taking a long look up and down at this overgrown young man, he said "Don't mind if I just call you mate, Boudreau." I've been paired with so many new lads, I get me own kids mixed up at home."

"Fine with me," Charlie replied, thinking it interesting that Louie felt he held such an upper hand.

"The long lines are coiled and the hooks and weights are ready for putting out," Charlie told him. "The dory's are clear of barnacles and their lines set."

Louie looked up at Charlie with astonishment and then down at his cup of coffee. How long had he been down here? Long enough for this bear cub of a man to do the work of two men several days at sea?

At 120 feet in length, this vessel, christened, *Goddess of Good*, had twenty dories (twenty foot deckless skiffs), hundreds of feet of line and thousands of feet of fishing line.

Just the weights alone were in the hundreds, not to mention the hooks.

Wondering about the abilities of his partner and possibly his own inability to keep track of time, Louie grunted a reply. "A mate worth his work, I've got," he grumbled and made his way upside to make sure they weren't farther from shore than he had thought. Sure enough, they had only been at sea a few hours. Shaking his head he looked east and took in the beauty of the ocean. Oh, how he loved being at sea. It was like the smaller the shore became, the larger Louie became.

Louis Ouellette was born in December of 1878 in a small unnamed village near Sydney, Nova Scotia. Owing his dark and strong features to his Native American mother and his gentle temperament to his father's French ancestry, he grew up mostly in the care of women. His father and all the other fathers were trappers and trackers and spent most of their time away from home. Close to the sea, his mother would take him sailing and fishing along the coastline to the north, through the maze of inland waterways natural to Cape Breton's landscape. From the time he was a child, Louis loved the sea. Now, more than sixty years later, he would always remember first his mother, when setting out. She had a respect and kinship with the sea, always yielding to the forces of nature and its' spirit. Louie hoped that this aggressive young lad was not too eager. Many a young man, too eager for his own good, never learned the lesson that came from his actions. Lying at the bottom of the sea, a boy gone on may have eons for his soul to contemplate, but no more the chance to redirect his course in this world.

They reached the grounds on schedule and took bearing for the first set. One by one the dories were lowered down to sea, followed by the crew of two per boat. Coiled at the bow in each dory were the long lines with the stern keeping hold of the hooks, weights and bait. It had been agreed between the two that Louie would sit bow, with Charlie at stern. Given his arthritis, it was an easy decision. Not only painful, it had robbed him of his dexterity and limited his skill at hooking and baiting.

Set out in series, they would float off one by one as the Captain pulled away allowing room for the rest of the fleet. A sail and mast aboard, reserved for necessary occasions, each dory was equipped two sets of oars, 50 pounds of bait, and a good measure of rum. Both Louie and Charlie were not given to drinking, save for the emergency need of warmth.

In time, the men in the dory would lose sight of the ship and as on this day, become enveloped in fog. Kerosene lanterns were aboard for night, although most relied on calling to locate their brethren dory men. Throughout the fog, after the lines and hooks were set to sea, the calls of the dory's could be heard back and forth across the Banks, fragmented like the echoed remembrances of a restless dream. Sometimes it was a banter of laughter and merriment, others a relay of information for the safety of the fleet.

Charlie and Louie loved the sea and although first out, they were bearing up well against the harsh winds and waves typical of the Banks in October. Waiting for the captain to return, they hauled in their catch and measured time with an hour glass, making notches in the gunwale for each turn of the sand. As the first boat out, a typical set and haul of the lines took a half-turn of the clock, six hours. At a little after seven notches, Charlie called out to the second dory to see if they had pulled up lines. They rocked back and forth and the sand continued to fall. At the ninth notch, they still had no reply. More calls were made, no answers were heard. The eleventh notch met the shackle for the oar. Louie lit the lamp in desperation and began calling out over and over, his voice rising to a shrill. Realizing they were no longer connected, but lost to the others, Charlie thought of all the past fisherman who were set out without a safety net; faithfully waiting for their captain to claim them before the sea could.

"No need to call, Louie," Charlie said. "Look at the gunwale, it's been too long."

"Oh, my God in Heaven," Louie replied. "I wonder how far off course we've gone?"

"No telling with the way she's been blowing," Charlie replied. "But, given the northwest heading, and a few hours drifting, I'd say we're no more than a tiny fish at sea, my man."

Having pulled-up a full catch, the two men looked upon the fish differently now. Before, they were fish -- an obligation to the captain and their crewmates and money in hand upon shore. Not more than a half-foot away in their little dory, they paid no attention to them other than to keep them in good condition. Now, as they lay in the bottom of the dory, steely cod eyes staring back at them, they were no longer just a possession, they were life, sustenance, and not much for the worse than the present state of Charlie and Louie.

Looking at each other, the men agreed to terms and the use of force upon another, if broken. They agreed not to drink the water. They agreed not to use the lamp, unless they heard an approaching vessel. They agreed not to eat the fish, until after four days. They agreed to regular rations of rum and to huddle for warmth. Most of all they agreed to stay aboard.

It was three days before they were rescued. The seas battered and tore fish, boat, and men. Bailing for hours and hours, Charlie kept time by notching the gunwale, reaching past the second oar in the last hours. A wash overboard took their lamp and most of the fish. Torn to shreds, the sail made little cover, leaving them exposed and freezing cold, their clothing wet to the skin. Huddled as low as they could, they called out names and stories to the wind to keep sane. Old girlfriends, cousins, people they loved, people they hated. The days of the week, months of the year, and rote nautical terms were sent over the wind and waves in hopes some kind of Goddess of Good, ship or no would save them.

After his second attempt to jump overboard, Charlie tied Louie to the stern. Making the knots tight, the old man bawled like a baby and Charlie cried for the first time, "To keep you from the sea and yourself," more to the sea than to his incoherent friend. Facing the violent and black abyss before him, Charlie screamed, "As for you, Mother of all seas, you'll not get us, you bitch. We'll walk on land again, if I have to row all the way there myself!"

As dawn broke and the sun began to give hint of its power, the seas lay calm and gentle, totally absent of the fury and menace it held before. A cold mist hovered just above the water giving it the appearance of fairy dust. At the stern, Charlie lay upon Louie holding fast to the oars. Frozen in embrace, he had been taking turns searching the seas and resting. It had been hours since Louie had moved and he wasn't sure if the old man had gone on or not. A faint sound circled around his outer ear and teased his brain into awareness. Opening his eyes, he was amazed, first by the gentleness of his hateful captor and then with great relief the familiar sound of a cargo ship. Tearing free from the icy tentacles that held them to the stern, Charlie stood up and began waving and screaming as best his frozen limbs and vocal cords could muster. Louie lay unresponsive. The ship was Norwegian and came upon them by chance. The dory had drifted into the shipping lanes just before dawn, much to their credit, for if at night, they would have been overrun for sure, left to lay at the bottom forever lost, only the sea knowing their fate.

Charlie bailed for the last time throwing a bucket full in Louie's face. The old man gasped and moaned. "He's still got some blood left yet!" Charlie rejoiced as he unloosened the binds that had kept him in this world. The ship dropped a rope ladder over the side, more than one hundred steps to rise. Throwing Louie over his shoulder, Charlie made the climb, happy for each pull of muscle, gasp for breath, each painful advance. Pain meant life and that was a hell of a lot better than the so called glory of death.

A couple of days later, Charlie was released from the hospital and made his way back home. He checked official records and no distress call had been given by the *Goddess of Good* on their behalf. A brief investigation was made and Bastardasche was free. No charges were made. Dock records indicated the catch was delivered without incident, a full twelve hours before they were rescued. Charlie never saw Louie again, but heard he spent several months in the hospital and then retired for good from the sea. As for Bastardasche, Charlie learned a good lesson. The true merit of a man is measured under the worst of events. Although abandoned by a much lesser man, Charlie now knew he not only measured up, but beyond.

RITA

Harsh Lessons

It was a typical summer Sunday morning. Sitting on a hard pew, the stiff creases of her dress pinching here and there, Rita was lulled to sleep by the soft chanting of Latin, yet pulled awake by the sweet nauseating perfume of her stepmother. Somewhere between the discomfort of her attire and the pendulum of her consciousness was the fear of being caught not paying attention. Stepmother was very strict about proper behavior in church. The way you sat, held your hands, even down to the casting of your eyes were under constant scrutiny. Yet, a second or two of too much reverence raised the suspicion of sleep which led to a quick hard pinch. Worse yet, was what came later, once home. Stepmother's wrath was neither to be escaped nor to be discounted. Stepmother was by all appearances a good woman. Not one to be described as kind or loving, her actions, at least those to others, showed a woman who took good care of her family. Quite handsome, large in features, given to fuller dimensions, she was a strong person in physical strength, presence, and of will and character. Stepmother was not to be toyed with. Yet, those in the church and neighborhood families believed she was a person to be respected. After all, when she married Frank, she took in Rita as if she was her own child.

With the sun beaming through the stained glass panels, Rita began to find it hard to stay awake. Every week they left early to get a seat in the first pew. Stepmother

43

wanted to be up front where she could see and be seen. The sweat began to trickle down her neck and pool where her stockings met the pew. Regardless of the temperature, a proper young lady wore stockings, a high neck dress with a skirt below the knees, and a hat. Although cotton was the fabric of choice, the sheer amount of starch gave the clothing a wallboard effect cancelling out any breathing the material inherited by nature. Then there were the shoes. Black and polished to a high sheen they were the latest in fashion for young girls. Making Rita the envy of the other girls, these shoes ensured that she would have no friends and yet at the same time reinforced the false impression of a loving Stepmother. And yet, should the purchase confuse Rita into thinking Stepmother may indeed love her, they were one size too small. The constant pinching of her toes kept Rita from wandering more than a painful step or two away and always kept her close enough to keep an eye on Ann.

Ann was her stepsister, six years younger than Rita and a daily reminder that Rita was always and only an obligation. Ann had beautiful chestnut hair and sparkling brown eyes and at the age of three held the heart of everyone that came upon her. Not one for cruelty, Rita loved her stepsister without reserve and often found Ann the only happiness since her father remarried. It had been five years since the wedding and at the age of nine, Rita really didn't remember a time when her Stepmother was not a cause for concern. Under the watchful eye and sidebar cruelty her

Stepmother delivered, Rita lived under a constant cloud of impending storm. Outbursts were redirected with closet confinement and the abstinence of supper. Protests and petitions to her father left only unanswered questions, followed by the pain of his absence and silence. Frank was like a ship loosing course at sea, his rudder holding to the way of least resistance, the way of little turbulence. Somehow knowing his course was set, Rita learned at a young age that she was cast to the life raft, adrift and alone in dealing with her stepmother. And although he loved her dearly, Frank would always cower and default under the pressures of his demanding wife.

After the death of Annie, Frank was in a casket of depression and despair. When the shock wore off and reality set in, he found it hard to perform even simple tasks. Things like cooking, cleaning, and the daily duties of the farm went undone. Hours would pass and Rita would be left alone in the cradle. Frank's mother, Nana, moved in with them to help, as long as needed. Nana was a widow herself, going on ten years, having lost her beloved to a sudden heart attack. A formidable woman, Nana took charge of any task requiring attention, requiring little attention herself. No taller than four foot six, she made up for height with speed, breezing through chores in the same time it took others all week. After the wake and funeral, Nana had returned home to gather her essentials and close up her house. Not a long distance, she was to return in three days time. When Nana arrived at the farm and found Frank sitting in the dark, cold supper from three nights ago on the table, and Rita wailing in her cradle she immediately went to the child. Gathering her in her arms and attending to her needs she said a prayer of petition for all of them, especially for Frank. With Rita settled, she turned her attention to Frank and in short order gave him the most scathing diatribe ever delivered, shamed him out of his inertia, and sent him off to confession for the good of his soul.

The next few years followed in regular routine. Frank worked the fields and took a second job. They needed the extra money and it kept him busy. Nana believed a busy body gave little time for reflection or contemplation which usually led one down the wrong path. Besides, Sunday was the time for reflection and contemplation – reflection of one's sins and contemplation of God's love and mercy. Rita grew into a chubby toddler and a somewhat demanding individual. On Sundays while Nana prepared supper, she would ride horsey on her father's knee, watching his solemn face slowly turn into a lazy smile and crinkly eyes. Should he lessen the trot or stop to rest, Rita would wail until the cadence was resumed. Frank could only please her, looking into her eyes for reminders of Annie.

"You're going to spoil the child rotten," Nana advised.

"Oh Mama, but she breaks my heart every time," Frank replied.

One Sunday afternoon, Frank took Rita for a ride in the wagon. They often took rides through the fields, and although working on Sunday was forbidden, this gave him the chance to truly appreciate his beautiful farm and view one of the many things he thanked God for that morning at mass. But this Sunday they turned onto the road and headed east towards town.

"Where are we going Papa?" Rita asked.

"I have a surprise for you, sweetheart," Frank said, giving her a wink and a laugh.

Dreaming of candy and ice cream or maybe a visit to the general store, Rita bounced up and down in her seat, giggling the whole way. When Frank turned into a homestead just shy of town, Rita began to pout. By the time they pulled in front of the house she was wailing "I want candy!" Frank tried to calm her down saying they would go to town, but she continued, becoming louder and louder, crying at full throttle. Soon, the whole family was on the porch gaping at the scene before them. A large woman with stern features made her way through the crowd to the wagon.

"Good Afternoon, Frank," she said.

With his head hung in shame Frank said "And to you, Mademoiselle Lorain."

Out of sight of the others and Frank, from her pocket, Lorain quietly withdrew a large piece of taffy, placed it in Rita's palm, and whispered "If you quiet down, the candy is yours, if not....." and her voice trailed off.

Rita immediately stopped crying, put the taffy in her mouth, and looked to her father for security with large pleading eyes. Not meeting her father's eyes, but that of the woman, she knew this was someone with whom you do not battle. As the wagon drove off and those on the porch waved good bye, the woman leaned toward Frank.

"Never give in to a child, it will always lead you and them in the wrong direction."

To which Frank whispered, "Thank you."

It was time to rise for the prayers of petition and Rita's feet were throbbing, her neck was itching, her stockings soaked, and her head pounding. Through all the discomfort she prayed for others: the poor and the sick and those who have left for our Father's kingdom. Her Latin was limited and she participated by rote in what she had learned through attending weekly mass. Stumbling over declinations and conjugations she tried to keep up and keep quiet at the same time. Not that Stepmother knew much about Latin either. Back in Canada she attended the same church as they did, St. Bernard's. There the mass was said in French. But here in the states, especially in Cambridge, it was Latin and Stepmother laid down the law that praying in French was not allowed. Rita shifted her weight from foot to foot to alleviate the pain. She lost her balance and fell into Ann who fell into Frank who fell out of the pew with a loud thump. Sheepishly rubbing his head, Frank rose and took his seat not meeting the eyes of others, helping Ann and Rita to theirs. Everyone quieted down and mass resumed. Ann buried her soft cries into Frank's shoulder as incense drifted around them. Left to soothe her own hurts, Rita dared a glance in Stepmother's direction only to see her profile in solemn attention to mass. Yet underneath the face of prayerful adoration she knew lied a truer face. One reserved especially for her and only for her. Rita prayed for redemption, she prayed to be saved.

Growing Up with Nana's Love

A child left to make sense of the harshness of one parent and the complete lack thereof in the other will try to cope through actions, generally not those preferred by adults. Not given to understand the power or use of words to express their concerns or even understand what they are experiencing, a child will act in any way to obtain attention – good or bad. In this way, Rita began to assert her will upon the unfortunate events of her life. As she grew into young woman, her years of conniving for love and refusing to accept that she was second or possibly third in her father's eyes, reinforced her belief that anything she desired could be obtained through any method regardless of moral acuity. In short, Rita got what she wanted at any and all costs. This was a reckless way to approach life under the stern eyes of her Stepmother and especially so at St. Patrick's Regional School for Girls. At St. Patrick's the order was both of St. Joseph and one of highest regard. Because she was a quick learner and a good student, the sisters had little opportunity to discipline. However, Rita's disposition was as unpredictable as the New England weather. With little indication of disastrous consequences on the horizon and an almost complete lack of knowledge of the forces of meteorological proportions at home, the poor sisters of St. Patrick's were often put to port by Rita's sudden tempestual changes. A learned manipulator from a young age, Rita was usually able to explain away the charges and keep a call from going home. In the event the call was inevitable, a quick run home and change of voice would put the matter to rest without Stepmother's knowledge. Survival for Rita was a skill earned over time, urgency being the key to her success.

It was the Feast Day of St. Patrick and a school day. The girls were allowed to forgo their blue unfashionable uniforms for an acceptable green dress, as the day would begin in church followed by a morning brunch celebration. Boston was true to its' Irish roots, not only in the pub, but at church as well. On this morning, the churches were full out the door with prayers to St Patrick. Ascending into the sunny skies, like a child's balloon too loosely tied at the wrist, the hopes and fears of that morning's faithful would echo through the parish reminding those not in attendance of their sins and faults, lack of convictions, and especially their poor chance of ever being saved by the graces of St. Patrick.

Stepmother was in favor of the green dress; however, she did not attend St. Patrick's on a daily basis, and never experienced the rebuke of those pure Irish Catholic Bostonian girls. It could not be held secret that Rita was not only not Irish Catholic, but she was not by birth American either. Born in Canada, she would remain to them so. Although an American citizen, who spoke English like a true Yankee, her French Canadian genealogy was as apparent as the nose on her face. Small and dark, Rita was in great contrast to her fairer, larger schoolmates at a time when differences were not favored. Given her disposition and will to overcome, this was not an obstacle for Rita, but a constant point of contention. In typical single minded fashion, Rita

51

obliged her Stepmother the green dress, albeit with her uniform underneath. The longer route to school passed through a wooded park, where the green dress would remain for the day.

Upon arriving at school, Rita quickly silenced any retorts from her classmates by placing a tag on her vest which read 'Pray for St. Patrick, for he is not French'. The girls took their seats in an unusually quiet manner. Noticing that things were not of typical order, Sister Mary took a quick look, settling on the only blue in a sea of green.

"Rita, come forward."

"Yes, Sister," Rita replied as she walked to the front of the room. Facing her peers, she was asked to explain the nature of her statement.

"It speaks for itself," Rita said.

Insubordination, indignation, disrespect, and nonconformity were the charges given. A call would surely go home this day, Rita knew. To make it home in time for the phone, the shorter route had to be taken and the green dress forgone. And just a green dress it wasn't. It was from Filene's in Boston. Stepmother had picked it out herself and spared no cost. Special occasions such as St. Patrick's Day were for showing off, especially for Stepmother in the eyes of the ladies of Cambridge. Not for the benefit of Rita and her social in congruencies at school, this dress and Rita's refusal to wear it, was a direct affront to not only Stepmother's authority but her very social standing in the community. Either way, Rita was to come up short. Neither willing to face the inevitability at home, nor the shame of returning to St. Patrick's, Rita purchased a ticket on the Boston and Maine. Bound for Nova Scotia and the arms of her Nana, Rita held fast to her prideful indignation and hope of salvation.

Nana was informed of her coming and waited at the platform. At first, when Rita did not come home a search was conducted and her dress found in the park. It had rained that afternoon and already nature had begun making the crinoline a home. No longer green, it appeared to have been host to a whole generation of boring and weaving organisms that found the netting a boon. Sergeant McNalley was assigned the case. Sgt. McNalley was a veteran of the Boston PD. A father of twelve, he had vast experience with youth and knew any event involving a young adult almost always was deeper than face value. However, not jumping to any conclusions, a muddy, wet dress in the park was just a muddy wet dress. A student of St. Patrick's not arriving at home from school was also just that. Not until he spoke with the Stepmother and the Head Mother would Sgt. McNalley begin to make connecting statements regarding the dress and the tardy student.

With no less than Broadway theatrics did the Stepmother confirm the dress in question was Rita's. With far less than vaudeville theatrics did Head Mother relay what had transpired in the classroom that day. Rita was last seen running out of the school building in the direction of town.

Sgt. McNalley, still shy of his fourth cup of coffee that morning, ignored the dull headache emerging at the base of his skull and called in a report to headquarters. Finding a young girl in St. Patrick's unfashionable ensemble should not be too hard, what with everyone loaded up in the churches and the pubs. Routine procedures included a call to all transportation centers in the city and sure enough the north station master had in fact sold a ticket to a young girl clad in the plaid of St. Patrick. A call was made to the stationmaster in Havre Boucher, Nova Scotia who in turn sent a young man out for a bike ride to Nana's farm.

Even a young, head strong girl, given so secure to her convictions will lapse in resolve after such an emotional event and a subsequent long period of time to reconsider. The trip to Havre Boucher was a long one. Tears long dried and anger long subdued left a young girl who was in dire need of love and reassurance. Shame and guilt were but a waiting room away and Nana knew a rebuke of any kind this far removed from the event would only do harm. One more enemy this child did not need. One more enemy would only ground her in her misconception of her righteousness. Not that she was all wrong. There were wrongs not of her doing, ones whose perpetrators should have the maturity and experience to know better. But, Rita needed to be accountable for her own transgressions, regardless of the complicacy of others. This was hard lesson for someone raised with the unfairness of life. Motherless, she lacked the unconditional love maternity affords. Never was an error overlooked or forgiven. Knowing doom is inevitable, the risk of throwing it all away pales as the lesser of two evils and caution is unheeded. But, Rita did have someone in her corner. Nana was there when she got off the train and for all the other trains Rita embarked to escape the unfairness and harshness of life. At least she had someone to run to – someone who gave unconditional love and support.

It was arranged that Rita would finish out her term by self-study. The summers would be spent at Nana's in Canada and in the fall they would return to Boston where Nana rented a small apartment near St. Pierre's where Rita would complete her last year of secondary school. St. Pierre's parish was more French than Irish and Rita fit very well into the classroom and the social scene. She would visit her Father on a regular basis, at his home or for dinner at the apartment. Although cold and detached, Stepmother had lost her reign over Rita and remained as absent as her father had once was himself. This was a special time for Rita. She had the easy love of her Father without all the conflicts of the past and the support and guidance of her Nana. Father would visit and they'd take long walks along the harbor, mulling over the ships, where they were from and what wares they carried. Frank dreamed of traversing the St. Lawrence Seaway. He told her one day he would take her on a cruise to Wisconsin. They would spend their days reading in the warm sunshine and nights dining and dancing to all the finest food and music. They talked about Annie often. The old wounds of grief had healed somewhat and it soothed

Frank to relive Annie with their daughter. Rita felt like he was living in the past, seeing Annie through her eyes and knew that these walks were probably the only happy times Frank could allow himself. He had tied himself to a woman who would not accept dreams, not of a past love, nor of any of the future outside of her own aspirations.

The sister's at St. Pierre's were impressed with Rita's intelligence and encouraged her to continue her studies. It was not common for a young woman in 1936 to go to college, but for a promising young student there were several women's colleges that were very well respected. A recommendation was given, an interview secured, and admittance accepted. Rita was going to study accounting. Her dream was to open a business, a café of sorts, where there was an abundance of good food, good company, and hard work. Rita had grown into a confident and gregarious young lady. Her restlessness was somewhat appeased with good hard work and the ethic to prove worthy of love.

CHARLIE

Flying the White Flag

From the beginning of the early 1920's, well into the 1930's there was a lot of secret spirited cargo below deck being transferred by Canadian ships to the US. These well compensated "spirits" carried a high risk when entering the US borders and many captains found themselves at the wrong end of bully club and suffered not only physical injuries, but delayed legal proceedings only to end up serving time in a dank and depressing cell. Prohibition was carried out upon the shoulders of America's social elite with a mission of no less than the perfect moral mission. Zealous about reformation, wealthy social ladies and their brethren male politicians, there were serious consequences to those who did not follow suit. Found with a hull of illegal, soul damming liquids straight from the devil, a Captain would end up either at the hands of thugs who carried out the dirty, but imperative social reformation with typical street fashion brutality or, probably for the worse, at the hands of a real reformer who would save souls at any cost.

After returning from a fishing run to the cap, Charlie made his way into the offices in St. Peter's to settle up payment with the owner of the boat, Mr. Flynn. Flynn was very happy with the numbers Charlie had been pulling in and wanted to keep the books building. The offices were far from fancy; actually, it was a series of dilapidated dockside shanties that had been slapped up next to each other. Sometime in the past, the roof was done over and the

58

exterior refaced to make it look like it was intentional; however, once inside the uneven floors and connecting door faces revealed the lack of vision. There was no central hall, but a connection that meant those in the front had constant traffic before them. Damp and cold, except for the occasional blast of heat given off by a random coal stove, made any person keep his visit short. A rise up the ladder of success was evident by horizontal ascension room by room. Mr. Flynn, having made his mark long ago, was at the end of the line and occupied the largest room.

"G'day Charlie," Mr. Flynn announced as he rose to full frame from behind his desk.

Tipping his hat, Charlie returned the greeting with a firm handshake. Back on Isle Madame, Charlie had been a giant to most, but here on the mainland where Scots had flooded the fishing industry he was met in height more often than not. Mr. Flynn was a fair but keen businessman, with the sense to use smarts & brutality where necessary. He too began his career as a young boy, working the lines on the old schooners, working his way up the ranks through hard and brutal work. Standing at six feet tall with the girth of two men, his stature gave credit to his Scot-Irish ancestors that settled in the northeast over 100 years before. His complexion was fair, one that bore evidence to many years of torment by wind, sea, and sun and sat in contrast to his short and wiry bright red hair. Reduced to its parts, he was not an attractive man; however, seen as a whole he was a great example of masculinity, strength and pride. Long ago confirmed a bachelor who jumped in and out of trouble with women, he was not always the hard & merciless moneymaker. A tender side was known by few, although it was a secret discredited by those who were more familiar with his iron grip of the fishing business. The two men stood dwarfing the desk between and regarded each other with a mixture of respect and wariness.

"Good run you had," Flynn said and gestured for Charlie to take a seat.

"The seas were with me this time," Charlie responded.

"It appears the seas are with you most of the time," Flynn said.

"Not counting any blessings; would be a fool to do so," said Charlie.

"Charlie, I like the way you work – you are tough on the crews and easy on the seas." Flynn began. "I have some cargo that needs to make it the states; it is a sensitive sort of cargo, if you know what I mean." It pays ten times more than what you're gettin now."

"I don't know much about running, sir," Charlie replied. "Not sure I want to either."

"Look, you make one run for me, that's all," Flynn offered. "I won't hold you to more." Then you decide – fishing or running."

At nineteen years old, Charlie was exceptionally young to be afforded such a dangerous and profitable offer. There was no question about Charlie's ability to carry out the transfer. A proven sea-worthy captain and not one for indulging in the bottle, he was just what Flynn needed. But at such a young age, there weren't enough years of experience for him to predict just how Charlie would react to so much money. Green with so much green was not always a good combination and Flynn didn't want to jeopardize the great loads of fish he had been bringing in with Charlie at the helm. And yet, something told him that Charlie was the man for the job. He'd been through a number of runners for captains and couldn't keep them for long. Either out of fear or weakness for the bottle they would disappear, sometimes stateside, leaving Flynn with the task of retrieving a boat under much suspicion.

Sliding a revolver across the desk, Flynn said, "Keep this at your side; it will keep the men in-line."

"Don't need a gun to hold my crew," Charlie said. "Never touched one in my life."

"This isn't fish, Charlie." Trust me," He said. "Take the piece and do the leg. A man named Smith is waiting for you; he's with Redmonger Fisheries." Rising from his chair he clapped Charlie on the shoulder and said "go easy on her" referring to his 80 foot steam trawler he lovingly called The Seawife. "See you back 'ere next week."

Taking hold of the revolver, Charlie emptied the cylinder. Leaving the shells on the desk, he turned to go.

"I'll take the gun, if that's what you want. But I'll run my crew like always. Not a one of them can swim and it's a long way to the bottom of the sea," He said.

With the cargo below and a fresh load of fish in the hold, the crew hired and the ship set for sea, Charlie took to the helm and led her out of port. It was early in the morning on the 1st of October. First light was beginning to make its way over the horizon, giving the surroundings a cold and steely grey look. With the wind in her favor, Seawife could top out at 11 knots, making her way into Boston in about 2 days. Although salted on ice, the catch had a timetable before it would spoil. Charlie knew he'd probably forgo sleep on this trip and wouldn't rest, mind or body, until he was back in Canadian waters headed downeast.

The crew was a mixture of knowns and unknowns. Most of them were family men who were daring enough and desperate enough to make the trip. Although, selling spirited cargo to the US was not considered illegal by the Canadian government, once inside the US waters, there was little their country could do for them. The first mate, Jonathan Donovan, a big second generation Scot from St. Peter's, was good to have aboard. A head taller than Charlie, the crew was under his watch in more ways than one. A shock of unruly red hair covered his crown and crept down to his chin forming a frame around his angular and strong face. Given to pull at his beard while deep in thought, Donovan appeared to be stretching his jaw open and closed in want of what to say. He was a quiet sort of man; but when he spoke it was worth listening.

Donovan took the helm after the first watch.

"Hey, Captain, take a load off and fill yer mug," Donovan said.

"Yup, I think I'll do just that," Charlie replied.

"Fair and easy weather so far," Charlie offered.

"Course is set, check her again at 1400," He added.

As Charlie made his way below deck, Donovan set his mind to the sea. Running a hand across his rough and wind beaten face, he tried to wipe away his unease about this trip. This was a first for him. He swore to Megan he'd never get involved in running; although many of their neighbors and friends had turned in need of cash. Times were hard and even with his luck of getting hired by Captain Charlie, who had the best catch record around; he still kept coming up short on funds. 'Tis' no surprise.' He could hear his wife saying. 'Every time you come ashore, I get another blessing.' She'd say. 'You'd have to fish all year long to keep this crew clothed and fed and that's with me sewing the clothes and milking the cow!' Ten blessings so far and he still couldn't keep his eyes off her. 'There's no stopping ya, Donovan' she'd say. 'God knows.' God, he hoped she'd never find out. She'd kill him or put him out to sea for good. He had a terrible feeling going behind her back; yet, if he could just get through this trip, the last one for the season, and then they'd have enough to make it through the winter

Pushing thoughts of home away, Donovan corrected their course, swearing to stay focused. Losing yourself at sea could cost a whole lot in terms of money and lives. Never one to mix fishing and family, this was a new feeling for Donovan. A true fisherman left the land on land and went to sea with only the sea. Carrying baggage from home was a sure recipe for trouble. Given the futility of worrying over troubles that will still be there when you land, it was best to leave them ashore. Looking out over the sea, the great swells seemed to move along without hurry. A lazy sea, they called it. Yet, experience told him not to confuse lazy with benevolence. Lazy could become angry in short order and the warning signs were there if one kept alert. Changes in wave length (crest to crest) or height (swell to crest) could indicate a waking and menacing sea. Noticing the barometer falling, although not too quickly, Donovan kept mindful of the maladies low pressure could bring out here in the cold grey waters.

The journey from St. Peter's to Boston was well traveled. Donovan had sailed this course many times and in his mind he divided it up into three parts. The first leg held Nova Scotia in sight on the starboard side. The second leg, after losing the lights of Yarmouth, out of sight of land was navigated by holding a due course southwest. The third and last part held a slight glimpse of Cape Cod to the bow, port side, until Boston began to make an appearance straight ahead with Portland and Portsmouth peaking out in a northeasterly fashion along bow, starboard side. Only then, could he imagine he could see the lights of Gloucester way to the north off the starboard side. There was a certain awe and respect given to the Gloucester Fishermen. Competitors on the Grand Banks, they were fierce comrades with which to contend. Beating the Nova Scotians on the great cod banks came with twice the peril. Coming from such a distance, they fought the Atlantic far longer than the Nova Scotians, having to reach the Maritimes and then traverse its' length before Donovan and his crew even threw off their lines.

Taking turns, Charlie and Donovan kept Seawife on due course. The lazy sea stayed true and even the westerly's that often slowed the approach was lacking in conviction. As the sun began to offer its full beauty to her surroundings, they navigated around Deer Island and set a straight course for President's run, leading into the harbor. The crew was on deck, ready with the lines. Donovan was port to the helm, heading forward when he heard the shouts aft.

"Vessel approaching stern, Captain!" Yelled one of the crew.

"How far off?" asked Charlie.

"Bout 100 yards, but closing in fast, what're we gonna do?" the crewman asked nervously.

"Looks to be a cutter, Captain," Said Donovan as he turned and made his way back aft.

"Raise the white flag and we'll hold course," Charlie ordered.

The white flag, although required upon all ships, was one you never wanted to have to raise. White wasn't surrender, but a warning, one that came without question. Tuberculosis. Fear. Death. Even the law wouldn't dare board a ship with a white flag. Even so, it was a ploy you could only use once and only in waters not familiar.

The cutter approached and sounded a signal, ordering the Seawife to neutral. Charlie cut back the throttle and held the bow against the tide while the cutter closed in. About 20 yards away the captain of the cutter identified himself and asked the Seawife her business. Charlie was about to respond when the captain of the cutter saw the flag and sounded a signal for her to proceed. The cutter quickly pulled away leaving Charlie, Donovan, and the rest of the crew to continue course – and to exhale.

"That was a close one, Captain," Donovan said. "My wife would have killed me if I ended up in cell in Boston."

"Big muck like you, Donovan, your wife wouldn't have had the chance," Charlie said. "Boston doesn't have any cells for rum runners, just coffins."

"Never again," Donovan said. "Just get me back to St. Peter, never again!" he vowed.

After unloading the cargo, both catch and cargo, and free to breathe easy, Charlie brought the Seawife home to St. Peter's and headed straight for Flynn's office.

"Made your delivery, Flynn," Charlie said in an even and no-uncertain-terms voice.

"Here's your money and your gun. I won't be running anymore, for you or anyone." He stood with his arms folded across his chest and held his voice even. "No amount of money is worth going to the dogs."

Turning on his heel he left the building as quick as he entered, leaving those he passed to stare in wonder and quickly discuss what happened. Flynn didn't bother to follow or ask. Although he never saw Charlie unleash his temper, he wasn't about to test him. Just like a seasoned captain, a good businessman knows when to cut his losses and move on. And move on they both did.

RITA

Meeting Raymond

A month before her first semester the fragile security that had been building over the last year came to a fault. Nana suffered a heart attack and it was not clear if she would recover. The physicians at Boston General were somewhat surprised she survived and gave credence to her stamina and positive perspective. Little did they know the strength this woman possessed. At 40 years of age, Nana was as powerful and full of life as a young woman. Having raised two generations, she would go onto to raise a third and enjoy the love of a fourth. However, at the time her heart was failing and Rita felt as if she had lost her moorings. All too familiar with the feeling of being adrift, Rita forwent her education and remained to nurse Nana through her recovery.

It was during this time that Rita began to reconnect with her step-sister Ann. Always devoted to her little sister, Rita still loved her as when she was young, but now the relationship took on new dimensions. With Ann approaching womanhood, she enjoyed new found freedom from her mother's iron grip. Although stepmother gave Ann an entirely different up-bringing, she was still a harsh woman with little room for forgiveness. Ann decided she was not going to be the victim any longer. Ann and Rita would meet for dinner at the apartment and often go strolling through the Harvard campus or catch a movie at the theater. City transport was convenient with rail connections and short walks to and from any destination. Boston was a pleasant city to dwell in the late 1930's and a safe one for two young women to explore.

With Nana in the hospital recovering, Rita had the apartment to herself and like any lively, fun-loving seventeen year old, she made the most of her time socially. A guardian of sorts was in place in the form of Mrs. Peabody, the neighbor. She would look in on Rita from time to time and make sure she was doing well, but this was a mere formality, because Rita was by all outward appearances a mature young adult. She worked the mornings at a local diner waiting tables and soon moved up to shift manager. Her ability to add large sums in a quick fashion and the accuracy of her tallies led her to handle inventory before the diner opened. This meant an early rise and her steadfast attendance to this made her all the more a responsible adult. Rita liked the restaurant business and began to see one within her grasp even without the college degree. She felt the satisfaction of a job well done and impatience of youth at waiting four years to end up at the same destination. Her evenings were spent at the hospital, checking on Nana's progress and assuring her that a trip home was coming soon.

Socially, Rita had a group of girls from the diner and a few from church with whom she spent time. None were any more special of a friend than another and they generally spent their time together on lighthearted, fun matters. Trips to the zoo or a picnic lunch in the park, dinner at a friend's house or an afternoon ball game were typical. There was a lot of laughter and a lot of watching the other groups of young adults, the ones who were also watching and laughing too.

It was during this time, on a beautiful, warm fall day, that Rita and her friends had decided to take a drive out to Cape Cod. The diner was closed on Monday and with Nana's return home in a few days, Rita took advantage of the time away. One of the girls borrowed her Daddy's Cadillac convertible for the day and that meant sun on your face and wind in your hair for an exhilarating ride to the coast. A deep mahogany red with a great wide chrome grill in the front, this two-door beauty glistened almost as much as the young beauties it carried. Rita had packed sandwiches from the diner, another brought the drinks, and others brought blankets, and games – it was to be a great time.

Driving along Route 3, headed for the Sagamore Bridge, a loud noise and difficult steering left the girls at the side of the road with only three good tires. Surrounded by marsh on either side for miles before the bridge, the girls exited the car and stood bewildered at their situation. Rita opened the trunk and located the spare tire and a jack. She removed her new bathing dress and down to her suit, quite a scandal the girls laughed, kneeled beside the car and began to change the tire. The rain from the day before, still clinging to the side of the road, made miniature pools of silt and stone. Working to free the tire, Rita's knees began to sink. One of the girls grabbed her around the waist to keep her from falling over. As the last bolt loosened, the tire spun free, as did the girls landing among the pools, ruining any party its' miniscule inhabitants had in store. In whatever haste typical to young men, a pick-up truck sped past, taillights glowed, brakes squealed and then quickly they returned to offer assistance.

"Well, will you look at that?" Raymond exclaimed.

Approaching the Cadillac, he said to his buddies, "I believe the lady has saved herself!"

Having secured the tire and returned the car to the ground, rising to meet him, Rita extended her hand, there on the side of the road, beautiful in her beach attire, grease and mud smeared on her knees and a little above her brow, and gave him a shake worthy of a man.

"And that surprises you?" Rita retorted in good spirit.

"I am always surprised at the sight of a beautiful woman, especially one brave and bold as you!" He responded.

"Well, you can return the favor if you wish, and join us."

Smiles from the girls and shouts of agreement and general roughhousing from the boys confirmed the day to be had. Racing along route 3, the beautiful Cadillac followed closely by the hardworking Ford pickup, they made way to a beautiful day on the shores of Cape Cod. Life would never be the same for either Rita or Raymond again. Bound together first by love and then by children Raymond would continue to follow in Rita's glistening beauty for the next 16 years.

The Match

It was a splendid summer. With Nana at home and back to running the household affairs, Rita was free to be young again.   A change in their relationship, since the role reversal of caretaker and dependent, had led to a more even field in authority between the two. No more the adult and child, they shared the tasks of adoration and concern for each other with respect and love. Rita knew her boundaries as a young woman should and Nana, although watchful, kept a watchful step away from immediate affairs.

Since that first day at the beach, Raymond had pursued Rita with more intensity than she was accustomed. Being of strong character, it was usually Rita who took the lead, ultimately ending with a hasty retreat of the one being led.   When there wasn't a retreat, Rita often became bored and would leave off without more than a word. Her friends said she would never marry, that her castaways and deserters would fill the pubs with tales until no man would dare to even say her name. Rita responded that if a man doesn't have what it takes to last a week or two, then what marriage would there be anyhow? This match of wills with Raymond was new to her and threw her perception off enough to hold her interest longer than usual – long enough for love to take root and for her Stepmother to take notice.

Although Stepmother had gladly side-stepped to allow Nana to raise Rita, by all social standards a wedding was in her area of concern -- as far as she was concerned. As her father, Frank would be footing the bill, and Stepmother felt any monies spent would be wise to raise their social standing. Such an opportunity could not be overlooked. And an improper wedding could do a lot of harm to all the hard work she had put in over the years in social affairs. Luckily, Raymond was from the right kind of family. Good, hard working, God fearing French Canadian families, the Forgeron's were well respected in Boston. More than seven brothers and sisters here and in Arichat and Halifax, Nova Scotia, the Forgerons and Melansons had followed similar geographical and social paths to the present.

Without knowledge of the two intended, Stepmother and Frank, led a little against his will, had several meetings with Raymond's parents regarding the futures of their children. Both families felt there was nothing in the two to cause alarm and genuinely liked the pair. Frank had spent many evenings chatting with Raymond, waiting for Rita, and felt the boy was a good natured and possibly willful enough to handle his adoring and precocious Rita. He hoped he would be a good influence on Rita, for although evenly matched for strength, Raymond's might ran on the side of genuine good where Rita's often ran random and sometime just for the spite of a good fight. Frank recognized the restlessness of youth in the two, reminding him of his courtship with Annie. Knowing how the future was so unpredictable, he gave his blessing and prayed for them. Stepmother never bothered with Raymond, other than to assure herself that the net social outcome would be in her favor, for gain was the objective. Unlike Frank, she did not concern herself with the wills of the two, or whether the match was good for anything other than her name. Confident of the latter, she used her usual method of bold social graces to push the intendeds to the altar even before it occurred to Raymond to ask.

The Forgeron's had also spent time with Rita and enjoyed her company. They felt she was a fun loving young woman with good morals and would be good for their somewhat wayward son. Seeing how intent he was on Rita, they decided to allow him latitude to see where this would go. Upon meeting with Rita's parents, they decided in favor of Frank's gentle manner and in spite of Stepmother's brutish charm, to agree to the match.

A match was made.

Wedding Day

It was a particularly cold day even for January in the northeast. Boston had had its share of digging out and winter wasn't even half-way through. Icicles hung on any precipice available and people drug themselves to and from their daily obligations like dark shadows in a world of white. Rita was sitting in her favorite chair, facing the arctic outdoor scene, but her mind was elsewhere. Today was her wedding day. By all accounts she should be happy. Isn't a bride supposed to be happy on her wedding day, she thought. It was Raymond's mood last night that caught her off guard. He had showed up at the door, acting like a stranger. Standing at the door with his hat in his hands, he hesitated to come in when she answered the door.

"For God's sake, Raymond, get in here or we'll all catch cold."

Raymond continued to hesitate and so untypical of Raymond, Rita decided to keep quiet and see what was to come.

Usually when Rita answered the door, Raymond would surprise her with flowers or candy, but it wasn't the gifts, it was the delivery. Making up for height, Raymond did with might. No sooner had Rita opened the door, and Raymond was sweeping her off her feet and singing some silly song. One time Rita answered the door and knowing his antics wasn't surprised to see the porch empty.

"Raymond," she called out, "If you jump out and scare me, I'll kill you!"

By the time she had folded her arms across her chest and set her mouth in a fine line, he came around the side of the house with a kitten no older than 2 weeks.

"For you, my love."

"Oh Raymond, she is so beautiful."

"I know," he responded, "That's how I knew she belonged with you."

Standing with the door between them, Rita was at a loss for words. Opening the door, he followed her into the living room where Rita took a seat on the sofa. A nice warm fire was blazing and Raymond remained, back turned to her, warming his hands. In the dimming light of the setting sun, red and orange blazed across the room illuminating the solitary figure by the fire, making him appear as if he was the source. The silence was deafening. Just as Rita was about to speak, Raymond turned. Tears were coursing down his face and with no attempt to hide them he began to speak.

"Rita, you know I love you. I am just afraid of failing you," he mumbled.

"I don't understand," said Rita.

"You don't realize what you do to me, do you?" he begged. "I have never been happier, and yet I feel as if it all is on stolen time. It's like the world is bright and alive with you; I'm so bright and alive with you, that it is too good to be true." He explained.

"Why would it end? I love you to," She offered.

"I don't know, but I feel like I won't be able to keep up or be all you want and maybe you are better off without me." He sat down on the couch next to her and put his head in his hands and began to sob.

Rita took a few deep breaths and chose her words carefully for once. "Raymond, I want the world, but only because of you and only with you. Don't leave me, I need you," She whispered.

That was the first time Rita had ever said she needed him. He wasn't so sure that she really did and that was what bothered him the most. If she didn't really need him, then what would happen down the road when their marriage became predictable? He wasn't sure he could keep on surprising her; keep on impressing her, so what happened then? Without answers to his questions he held onto to her reassurances with the faith of someone with their whole life ahead of them. She held him in her arms until the fire descended to embers. With the cold creeping up on them, she kissed him on the forehead and walked him to the door. A smile appeared on his face, a transformation restoring the Raymond she knew and loved.

"See ya in the morning, young lady," He sang and off the porch he jumped with a kick of his heels, placing his hat on his head he sang "No more goodbyes tomorrow, only hellos for us...."

A ring of the doorbell broke Rita from her thoughts of last night and hearing laughter and the tramping of many feet she stood up and squared her shoulders. Looking into the mirror she realized that Raymond wasn't the only one with doubts and fears. That was probably more of her dismay this morning than anything. Nonsense, she thought. Everyone has wedding jitters, why should I be any different? Quitting was not something Rita did. And with their whole lives ahead of them, they had every reason to be happy. Smoothing back her hair from her face she turned to go downstairs.

"Rita," her cousins called from the kitchen, "Get down here; you are going to be late!"

"I'll be right there," she called.

And to herself she murmured, Raymond, I'll always be right there.

Diane

The room was warm and bright. The stark white walls reflecting light from the ceiling and windows, made it appear as if she was floating. As her vision cleared, Rita knew where she was, but confusion lingered. A soft touch on her shoulder and a turn of her head brought to view a warm smile and matronly assurances that she would be here soon.

"You had a hard time, dear, but everything turned out okay," The nurse said.

Images of being wheeled in the room and hands helping her began to surface.

"It's the ether, leaves you a little confused. It will pass soon."

Again the nurse. A cry, small and soft, coming closer and closer. This time a different nurse, warm and friendly, and a tiny bundle for her to see. Pulling back the blanket, she held her breath – a baby girl. Beautiful, brown eyes drew her in, looking back at her like she was physically connected. The tiny fists holding tight to an invisible string, her head moving a little away, Rita said "Oh God, look how beautiful." The eyes turned back and looked deep into her again, knowing this voice, recognizing the mother from within.

It was a warm winter inside with the love of Diane. New parents and grandparents make for struggles, yet Rita and Raymond felt blessed and normal annoyances seemed insignificant. Already Diane was six weeks old and spring was trying to make its way past a lingering winter. Cold and crocuses merged, singing birds and snow showers coincided, and sunshine warmed the cold ice holding fast to anything solid. It had been sometime since they had been out visiting and so they planned their Sunday with morning mass and brunch with Frank and Ann. Stepmother was busy elsewhere and Rita was not disappointed. Her new status as mother had brought a truce between the two women. Diane was a wonder and any past grievances paled in her presence.

With the birth of Diane came another blessing. Nana came to stay with them. Still very much an independent woman, Nana came for a few months. In the summer she would return to Canada. Nana was reminded of when she came to help Frank with his little girl and how Diane was so like Rita as a baby. The dark hair and eyes, the tiny mouth, were all so familiar. Diane was an easy baby to care for and her temperament made her all the more endearing. With two women, the house was clean, the dinner made, and the baby fed and changed without much fuss. The best was sharing the wonder of a new child with her grandmother. Rita was once again surrounded by the love she so needed, unconditionally, now from her child and again from her grandmother.

With the baby bundled up and the car warmed up and the bottles put up the three of them set out for mass. It was the first time they brought Diane to church since her baptism. Such a good baby, there was no worry about her crying or disturbing mass. The music was beautiful and Diane cooed and giggled when the organ played. On the way out of church Father McDonald gave Diane a blessing and congratulated Rita and Raymond.

"So, she takes after the mother, doesn't she?" Father observed.

"God is wise, isn't he?" Raymond retorted.

"Wise enough to know where to place his blessings, he is," Father answered playfully.

Nana laughed and said "All babies are beautiful." To which Diane began to cry and cry and cry.

The smells of breakfast were overpowering and the café a little on the warm side. Nana unbundled Diane and gave her a bottle. Little noises came from the bundle and brought smiles from the waitress as she took their order. Quite a way along she was, the waitress rested her pad on her belly and waited for their order. Raymond ordered a full breakfast of steak and eggs, coffee and toast. He was an eater of big proportions, quite inverse to stature. As lean as he was, it was a wonder where all the food went. Nana ordered oatmeal and coffee, her constitutional breakfast, and Ann requested coffee only, black.

When the waitress looked at Rita to take her order and she paused "Dry toast and coffee for you?"

83

A conspiratorial look crossed Rita's face and with a slight hue of green she nodded in agreement. Nana began to laugh and hugged Rita. Ann giggled and hugged Rita too. In the squeeze between, the nipple of the bottle dislodged and Diane began to scream. More laughter was met by Raymond's dumbfounded and bewildered look at his family.

"Have you all gone mad?" He asked exasperated at the scene before him.

The women laughed harder and harder until tears of laughter had them reaching for tissues.

"Looks like God is giving you more blessings, Raymond!" Nana said. Raymond looked at Rita. She smiled at him, placed her hand over her mouth and ran to the ladies room.

"Oh, my God! Here we go again," Raymond exclaimed.

Janet

By the time Janet was two, Nana was living all year with Rita and Raymond, except for the summers. Summer was for Canada. Nana knew that they all needed a vacation from each other and it was a good excuse to visit with old friends and family back home. And while things in Canada were pretty much the same as ever, it wasn't the case in Boston.

Boston in 1947 was a time of great vitality. The war was over, the boys were home, and life was grand. Everything seemed more alive. People were happy and at last, the nagging fear that pervaded every war day was gone. People could breathe without worry; shoulders could finally relax now that the burden of war was gone.

Nana felt the relief of the post-war Boston, but it was in Canada that she could really relax. Life there was almost untouched by the rush to breathe, to do, and to live. The vibrancy of life in Boston was an affirmation of post-war exuberance. Rita and Raymond jumped right in, joining the picnics at the park or parties that ran well into the night. Rations were no longer and dressing up to socialize was fun again. Diane and Janet missed Nana when she left for Canada, but typical of kids, they stopped asking after a week or two.

When Diane and Janet were old enough to spend summers away from home, they began taking the train to

Canada. Nana had a trailer on a piece of property in Pomquet, Nova Scotia. It was a small piece of land, locked in by others. However, the others were family and what a great time they had. In Pomquet, almost everyone was a relative and if not related, then for sure by marriage. A troop of kids showed up each afternoon to play, chores done for the day. Hayrides and trips to the river to swim or dig for clams lasted until Nana called for supper. Sundays were spent at mass and then visiting family and friends.

One of their favorite things to do was visit Aunt Mary. Aunt Mary, their mother's cousin, was married to Fred and lovingly referred to as Mary-a-Fred. This namesake binding the husband and wife was never more fitting. Their home was one of fun and laughter, love and happiness.

Even for young American city girls, the novelty of long summer days in rural Nova Scotia began to wear off. Left to their own devices, Diane & Janet often came up with great plans to surprise Aunt Mary. The problem was Aunt Mary rarely left the farm. So, together with Jeannie their cousin, they would plot and plan for when the opportunity arose. Sure enough, one morning Aunt Mary announced she was going to town. She left a list of chores, but after that they were free. She warned them to watch out for the boys though; they had been target practicing all week and she wasn't sure the target was needed. Already they had shot out the windows in the shed and were told to keep to the barn and far away from the hen house. "The last thing I need is a skewered hen!" she declared.

With the house swept and the potatoes peeled, the girls donned aprons. Janet gathered the ingredients as Diane began creaming the sugar and shortening.

"We haven't any eggs," Janet said. "How can we bake a cake without eggs?" she asked.

"No problem," Jeannie said. "We'll just check the hens. All we need is two."

"What about the boys?" asked Diane. "We've got to pass the barn to get to the hen house."

"I'll yell out a warning," Jeannie said. "They won't be happy, but that's just too bad."

The first trip out to the barn, the boys said "Aye, go ahead." and halted their practice. Unfortunately, there were no eggs. So, back to the kitchen they went. By the third and fourth trip, the boys were groaning and the hens were getting ruffled. Still, there were no eggs. The girls kept running back and forth, the boys kept complaining at the interruption, and the hens kept up a chorus of cackling protests, until finally the eggs were produced. Just as Aunt Mary came in the door, the cake came out of the oven.

"Surprise!" They yelled and fell into their chairs laughing.

"Ten times," the boys complained about the girls going back and forth.

"Twenty at least," the girls claimed they had lifted the hens.

"Delicious!" Aunt Mary declared.

CHARLIE

Leaving Home

It was a long time before Charlie returned to the States. His experience raising the white flag put his mortality into perspective and kept him closer to home. In the years following he found love and married. On what seemed the most beautiful day ever, Charlie held his baby daughter for the first time. Never did life feel so wonderful. Holding Claire was like going to the moon, something every seaman dreamed about, especially when at the helm at night.

Charlie continued to make a living fishing, from trawling to long-lining. As the years passed, the vessels changed and so did the fishing industry. What was once a laborious process to off-load his catch, employing baskets by the hundreds, filling and carting them to the shed was now accomplished in a few strokes with new hydraulic machinery. The sooner the catch was off-loaded, the sooner back to sea. In the 1950's the Grand Banks saw the appearance of foreign trawlers, some as far away as Russia, better refrigeration, and more accurate navigational aids. More vessels, better equipped for the voyage and large holds meant more fish caught more often. It also saw the gradual depletion of fish. Still a decade away from the peak of cod catches, the future of the Grand Banks fishing industry was in peril. What was once a beautiful and very human experience, subjected to Mother Nature's timetable, a partnership of man and sea both of respect and awe, now became more like a fight with man trying to dominate the unpredictable and often uncooperative sea. Gasoline and diesel powered vessels replaced the graceful schooners of the past, along with machinery doing the work of ten men at the dock.

It was on an unusually cold October day that Charlie realized not only had the fishing world around him changed, but so had his marriage. He still had Claire and felt like nothing was better than spending time with her, but as a young woman, she had her own life and interests. She had found love and was to marry in the summer. She had chosen a good man, Eddie, and Charlie felt she was safe and secure. He loved his wife, but years at sea had caused a drift between them, one that no amount of steering could close.

Three months shy of his 30th birthday, he decided to take up an offer to captain a boat to the States. A seventy-five foot trawler was at the dock in St. Peter's with a full hold of cod. Bound for Boston and better market prices, it had been delayed. The captain to deliver the load was found dead in his cabin that morning. The same age as Charlie, he seemed full of life and good health. Little known to him, his heart was slowly giving up and while asleep, it seized. Never more did living life to its fullest seem necessary to Charlie. Taking the helm, Charlie left St. Peter's and took his heart with him. As he pulled away from the dock, throwing back the lines of a lost love, he set his course ahead. Not once did he look back, the future was before him, like the open sea, full of possibilities, and maybe even love.

RITA

Meeting Charlie

It was the 3rd time that morning the door had stuck open when a customer came in the diner. Like cows to the barn, Rita thought, not even enough sense to close the door behind them. Wiping her hands on her apron, Rita moved out from behind the counter and walked toward the door. March was the worst, she thought. At least with snow there was something pretty to look upon. It was kind of magical, the way it covered all the ugly and made the harbor look like a postcard. *Greetings from Boston Harbor*, it would say and all the lines on the ships would shine like diamonds. Hardly a postcard now, she thought. Cold, rain, and wind was a sure recipe for foul moods and fisherman seemed to be good carriers of the disposition. Not that all fisherman were alike. Far from it, for sure, especially when you counted in McFarley. McFarely had to be the happiest and funniest man alive. Just hearing him shout "Top of the morning," on his way in for coffee was enough to make her smile.

Closing the door, Rita took a look around her and thought about how lucky she was to have this diner. It wasn't anything fancy, but it had a long, bright red counter with twelve matching stools, ten booths along the windows that sat four, well two fishermen each. The kitchen ran the length of the back of the building, leaving enough room for storage, cold & not, and all the supplies needed. There were constant repairs, between the ceiling and the plumbing, but the location was perfect.

Boston Harbor was a big place and had room for many diners and taverns. But Rita's diner was right next to the weigh-in. The first thing a fisherman did when he came ashore was ready the catch for the weigh-in. The second thing a fisherman did when he came ashore was to get his pay, and the third was to look for good food and hot coffee. Rita was a smart businesswoman. She knew to have a successful business you had to offer what a person wanted, but also what they needed. Even better when the person you are offering to just came into a load of cash. Fishermen wanted hot, good food and after a long time out at sea, they needed it. When they came ashore her diner was the first welcoming sight they saw. It just so happened it had great service and great company too.

Having learned the business as a young woman, Rita knew you needed to work fast and efficiently to survive. But she also saw the need for customer service. Doing it all, yet acting like you had all the time in the world to talk with the guys was a task she mastered well. Serving a full crowd, keeping the cook on his orders, and still shooting the breeze with customers was her specialty. Fast, hot food was what a cold fisherman needed and plenty of it too. Rita had all the skills to keep her diner running as quick to time as could be. Her customers were happy and kept up regular appearances. But her warm smile and infectious laugh was the topping of it all. A fisherman had to be a hard sort of fellow, rough around the edges and not too easy on the feelings of others. But taking a break on shore, it sure was nice to see a pretty

94

lady serving up great food. Being beautiful didn't hurt either. Rita was a sight for the all too sore eyes of a fisherman, but as easy as she was on the eyes, she was hell on hearts, at least, until she met Charlie.

Rita retied the apron around her midriff and took a peek outside. There was a big crowd at the weigh-in. Given the nasty weather outside it was going to be a busy morning. It was three months since John decided to head back to Florida. John had started the business, but wasn't too good at keeping the details straight. He hired Rita because she was a hard worker who left nothing amiss. And nothing was amiss after the first week. The diner ran smoothly and John had time to sit back and chat with the customers. He was an easy sort of fella that could talk it up with anyone. But his mother took sick and needed him home. John wasn't sorry to leave Boston, although he liked the people, he hated the cold. Lucky for Rita, John had more money than he could count and he offered her a long term loan. Now this place was hers. It was her safe haven, free from trouble and captain of her own ship. Yes, she thought, I am lucky here, now if only I could be so lucky at love.

Rita and Raymond had been having trouble for a few years, but neither wanted to face it out in the open. Always ready for a fight, they piled squabble upon squabble until they weren't even sure what they were fighting about. They both knew they were mad, had resentments and hardships, but every time they tried to clear the air it ended badly. It was like love was not enough. Not enough to make Raymond understand why Rita needed the diner. Not enough to make Rita understand why Raymond needed her home. Raymond felt like she wanted more out of life than he could give her and why shouldn't she be happy with what he had given her? Rita did want more and felt that if Raymond loved her enough he would support her ambitions. Rita felt betrayed. Raymond felt abandoned.

Nana had been spending more time in Boston with them now that Rita was at the diner full-time. Diane & Janet felt the love and security of a good home, but Rita knew Diane sensed the trouble. If only she could protect them from the angst of a troubled marriage. It was unheard of to divorce your husband and raise your children alone. It was unheard of to divorce. Most families just lived in the war-zone and pretended that things were fine. Rita had lived in a war-zone most of her life and wasn't about to start pretending now. Not sure what to do, she did what she knew how to do. Rita went to work.

Making her way back behind the counter, a cold rush of air assaulted her legs. Stiffening against the cold she heard McFarely holler "Hey mate, close the door." Amen to that she thought. With her back to the door, Rita began refilling the coffee urn. Behind her she could hear the newcomer settle onto the stool and strike up a conversation with McFarley. She didn't recognize the voice, but it wasn't unfamiliar. He was a down-easter for sure, heavy on the" d" and short of the "th". He sounded like her relatives from Cape Breton.

"How's it going, mate?" she heard the newcomer ask.

"Ok, captain," McFarley responded. "How long ya been out?"

"Ah since the first of February; caught a whole mess a cod. Had to come in, the hold 'twas full," He said.

"Did ya get it weighed yet?" asked McFarley.

"Sure did, never leave the ship till the hold's weighed. Good way to get a light load if ya do," He said.

"Hey McFarley," someone yelled from the stool at the other end of the counter, "you know all about being light in your load don't cha?"

"Every mornin' for sure," McFarley laughed, "But Rita sets me up with her coffee. Hey, Cap't, so what was it worth?"

"Oh, bout thirdy three thousand pounds, biggest load so far."

"You do any fishin, mate?" Charlie asked.

"Who me?" McFarley asked. "Yeah, sure, all da time, worked most the boats round here sometime or other."

"Well, nice to meet ya, name's Boudreau, Charlie, and I guess you're McFarley," Said Charlie.

Rita turned around and filled their cups. She took a long look at this oversized fisherman. He had to be the biggest one to come in here yet. Not necessarily tall, but just big. He had short black hair with grey making it way about. His hands were strong and tough and looked like they'd been fishing since he took his first breath. Rita had seen her share of fisherman, but the eyes on this one looked friendly. He had a firm mouth set upon a strong and serious chin. He had the look of someone who could break your arm as easily as he could gently hold your hand.

"Boudreau, eh? I knew some Boudreau's." She smiled. "Let me guess, Cape Breton?"

A big grin broke out upon his face, lighting up his blue eyes, making little St. Nicholas crinkles in the corners. Oh boy, thought Rita, this is one big teddy bear.

"D'Esscouse, you know the place, eh?" Charlie asked.

"Sure, been to Arichat a few times, other side of the water. Sure is pretty up there," She said.

"So what brings you down here, never seen you before, Mr. Boudreau," she said.

"Oh, I've been out awhile now, since February. I was catching for Delong," he said.

"Well, welcome to Boston, Captain Boudreau," Rita replied warmly.

Turning around she caught her reflection in the mirror. She was smiling, a real smile. Well, look at that, would you? She thought. I've missed you, she said to her reflection, haven't seen you in a long time.

Over the next year Charlie found more reasons to come to Boston Harbor, but there was only one reason he came to the diner. He found himself drawn to Rita and liked the easy discourse of their relationship. He found himself falling in love. She was a challenge for any man, but she was worth the fight. For a man to spend a life at sea and have a happy marriage the wife had to be an independent sort of person and independence was at the very core of Rita's character. They were both secure in their lives with work and family and neither seemed a threat to the other. Love began to take root and what was once pleasant conversation over coffee became serious discussions. "You" and "me" became "we" and "us". Rita knew she was falling in love, but this time it was different. It was so easy to love Charlie. Rita felt like she'd never been this happy. All her life she had fought for the right to be loved, having to settle for second place. Rita found her moorings in the steady and true ground of Charlie's heart and being first for the first time, she'd discovered she'd do anything *for the love of Charlie.*

Neither being good at remaining in idle, they decided to make a change for love. When Claire was eighteen and Diane was twelve, Rita and Charlie dissolved their marriages of distress and pledged their love with the vows of a new beginning. For the next fifty-six years their union was a blessing, not only for themselves, but for everyone who loved them.

Acknowledgements:

To my Grandmother, Rita, I owe the appreciation of a life full of tenacity and vitality and the understanding of deep moral character – and of course predicate pronouns and dangling participles.

To my Grandfather, Charlie, I owe the desire to dream big, especially when it comes to love – and of course how to pick your horse.

Author's Note:

It was not my intention to write a historically correct fictional novel about the lives of Rita and Charlie, let alone a non-fictional account. Many of our family stories have become fictional themselves in the retelling, even when told by those involved. If the reader finds this story historically incorrect, I apologize, if in doing so it distracts you from the real purpose behind this book. It was my intention to tell a story that in reading you would come know the true character of Rita and Charlie. By crafting a fictional tale, I could relay all the things I so loved about them through situation, character, and plot. The theme is what we all strive for: Love -- in this case, _For the Love of Charlie_.

Made in the USA
Charleston, SC
13 November 2014